I0648694

War departement, Surgeon General's office

# Medical history of the War of the Rebellion

Water color drawings to illustrate fluxes and fever

War departement, Surgeon General's office

**Medical history of the War of the Rebellion**
*Water color drawings to illustrate fluxes and fever*

ISBN/EAN: 9783742821225

Manufactured in Europe, USA, Canada, Australia, Japa

Cover: Foto ©Andreas Hilbeck / pixelio.de

Manufactured and distributed by brebook publishing software
(www.brebook.com)

War departement, Surgeon General`s office

**Medical history of the War of the Rebellion**

# ORIGINALS of the CHROMOS

## IN THE

## Second Vol. Medical History.

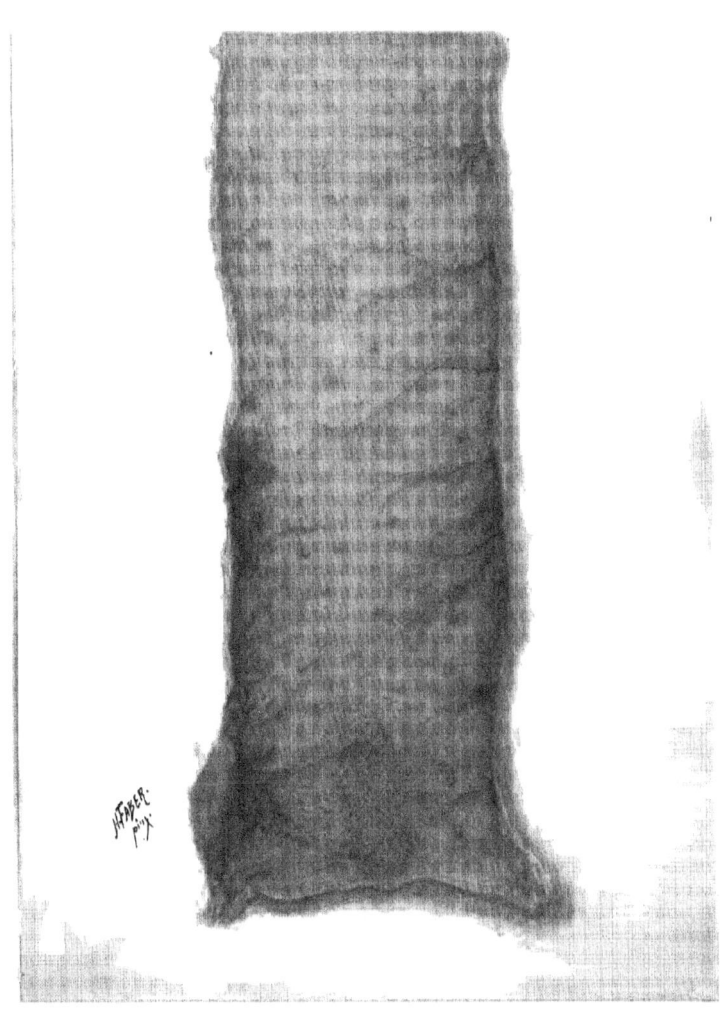

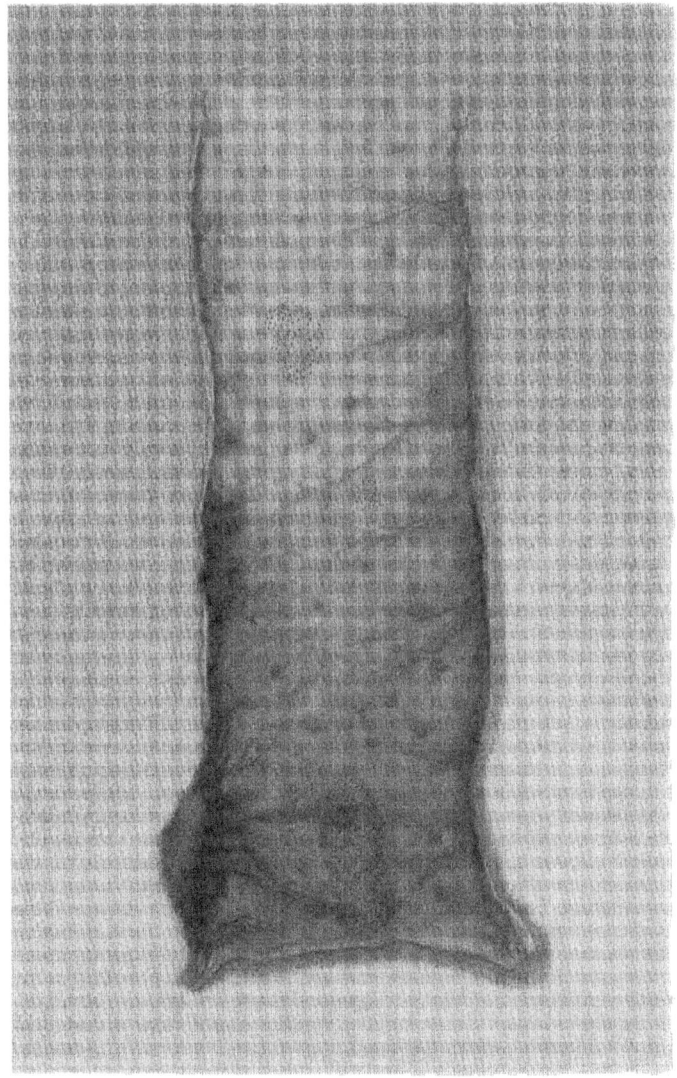

H. Faber pinx?       T.Moras chromo lm Philt

PORTION OF ILEUM WITH INFLAMED MUCOUS MEMBRANE,

solitary follicles enlarged, and shaven beard appearance of Peyers patches.

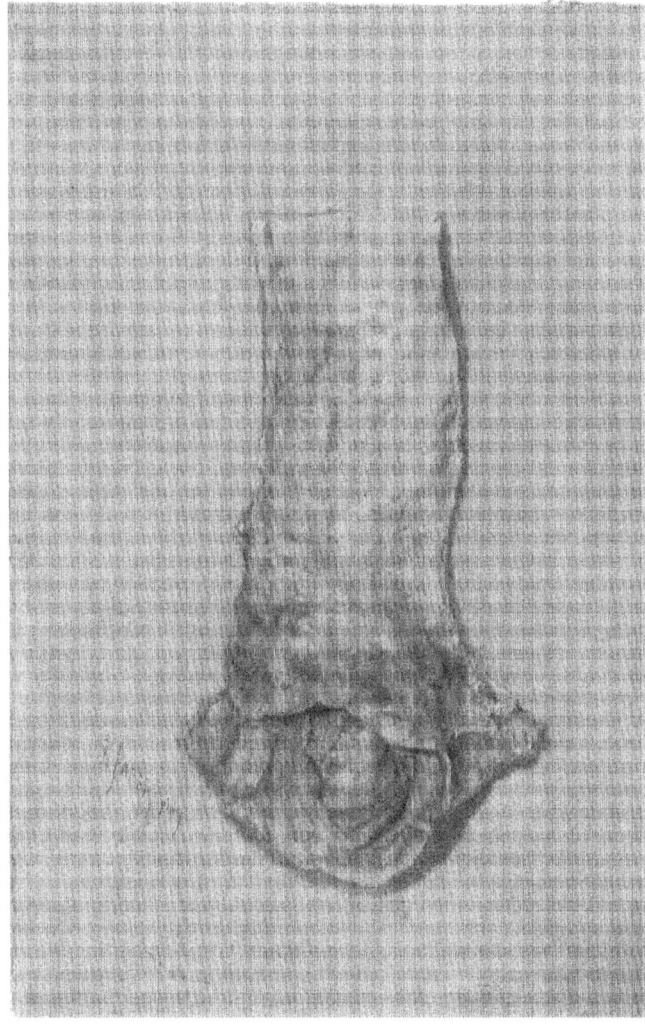

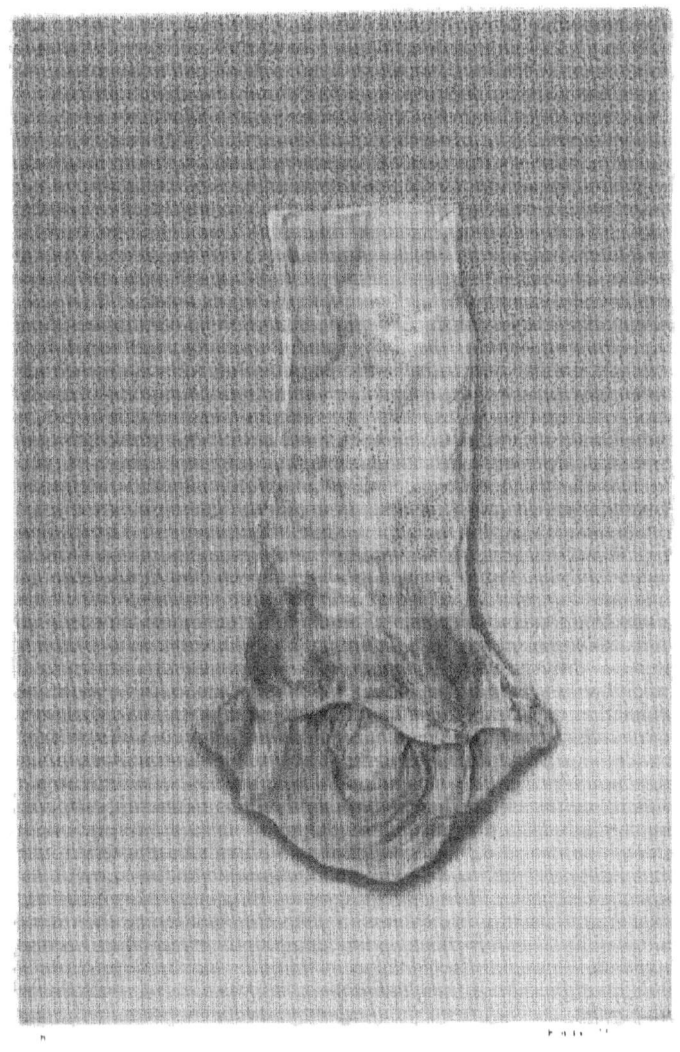

ANTEMORTEM CHANGES IN FECAL MATTER
near the ileocecal valve. Observational occurrence

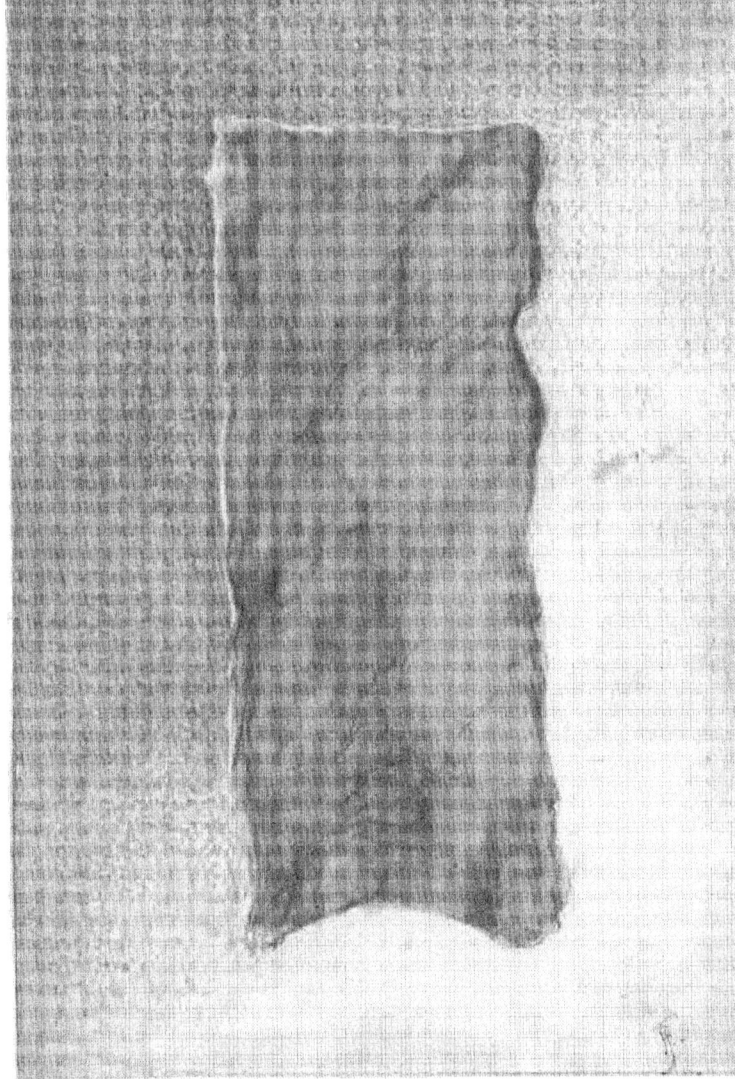

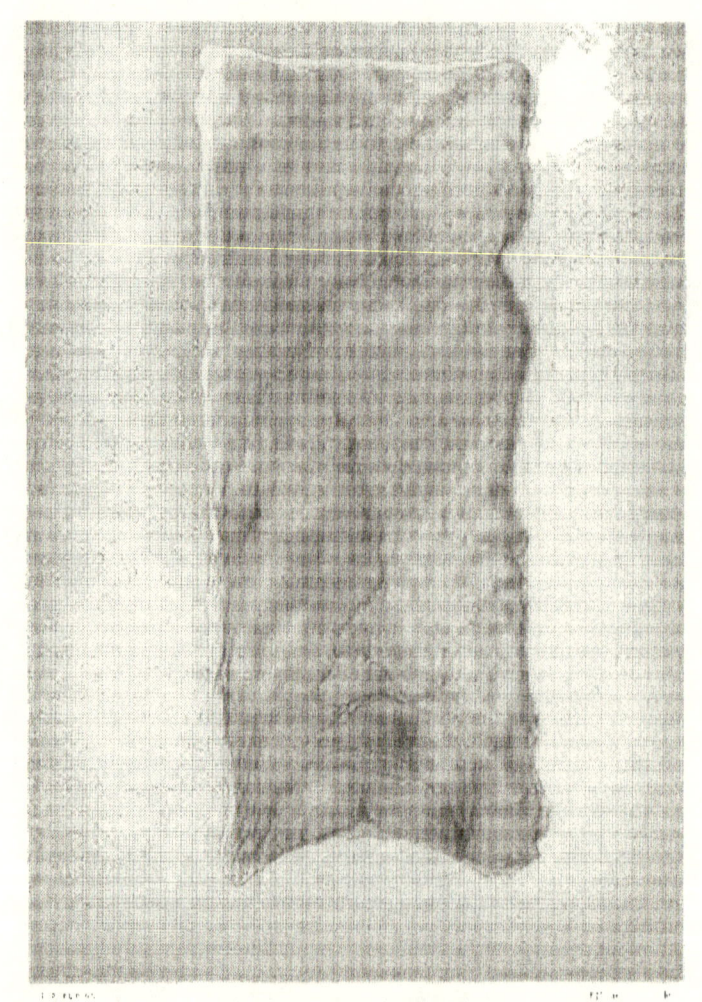

COLON WITH PIGMENT DEPOSITS

in and around the solitary Glands   Dysentery

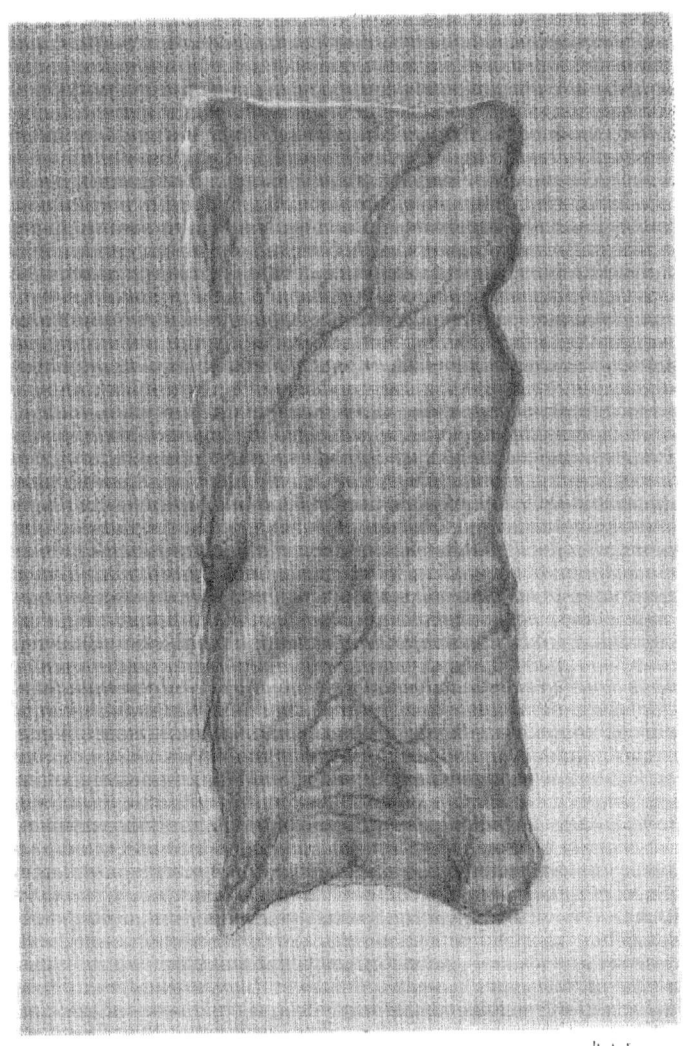

COLON WITH DIVERTICULOSIS

Br. and ground floor view, coal.

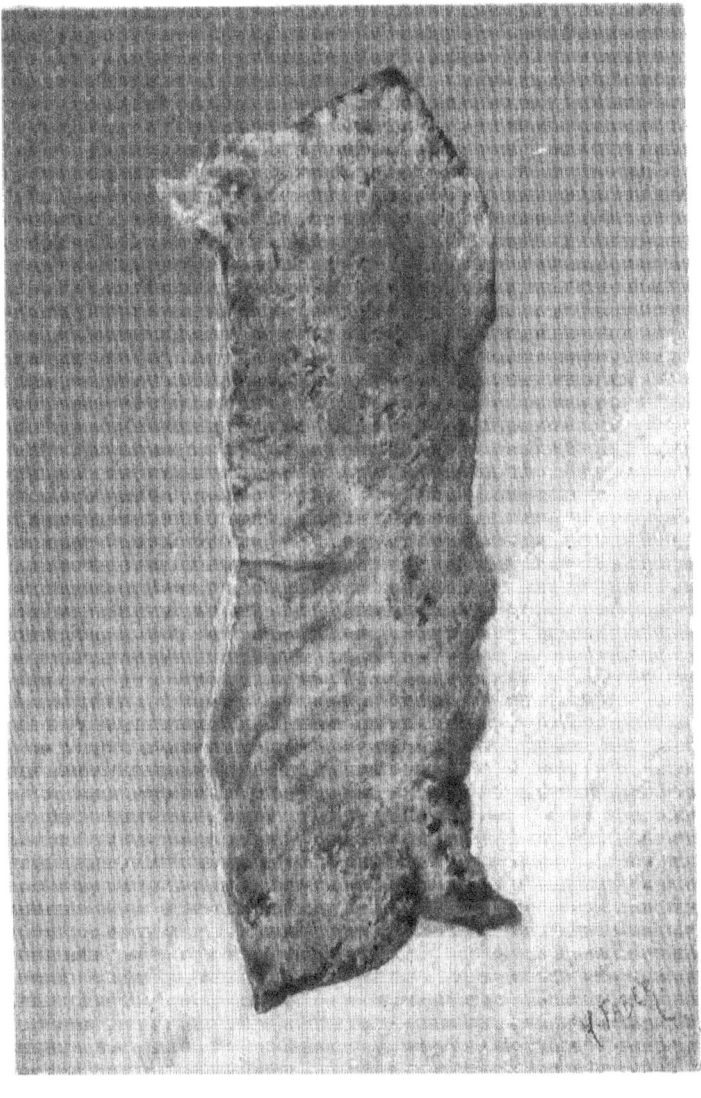

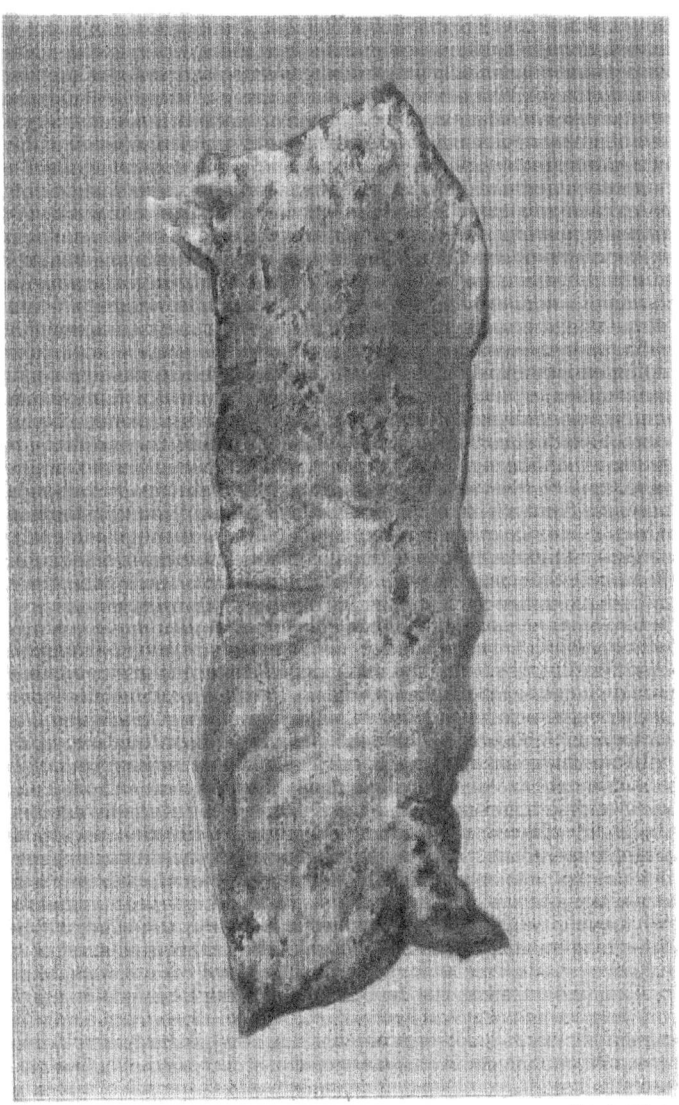

PORTION OF DESCENDING COLON,
coated with pseudo-membrane.

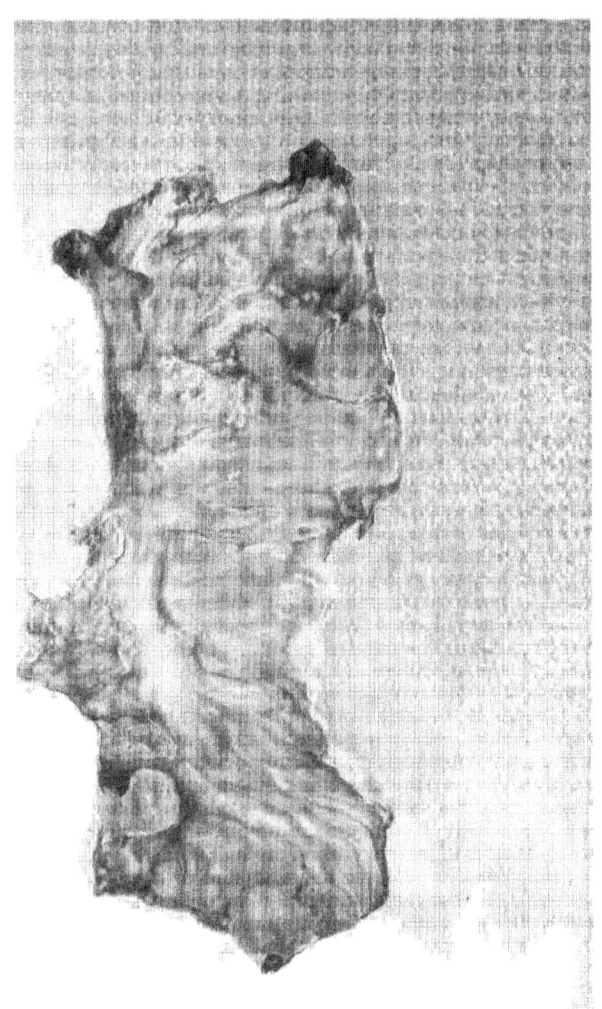

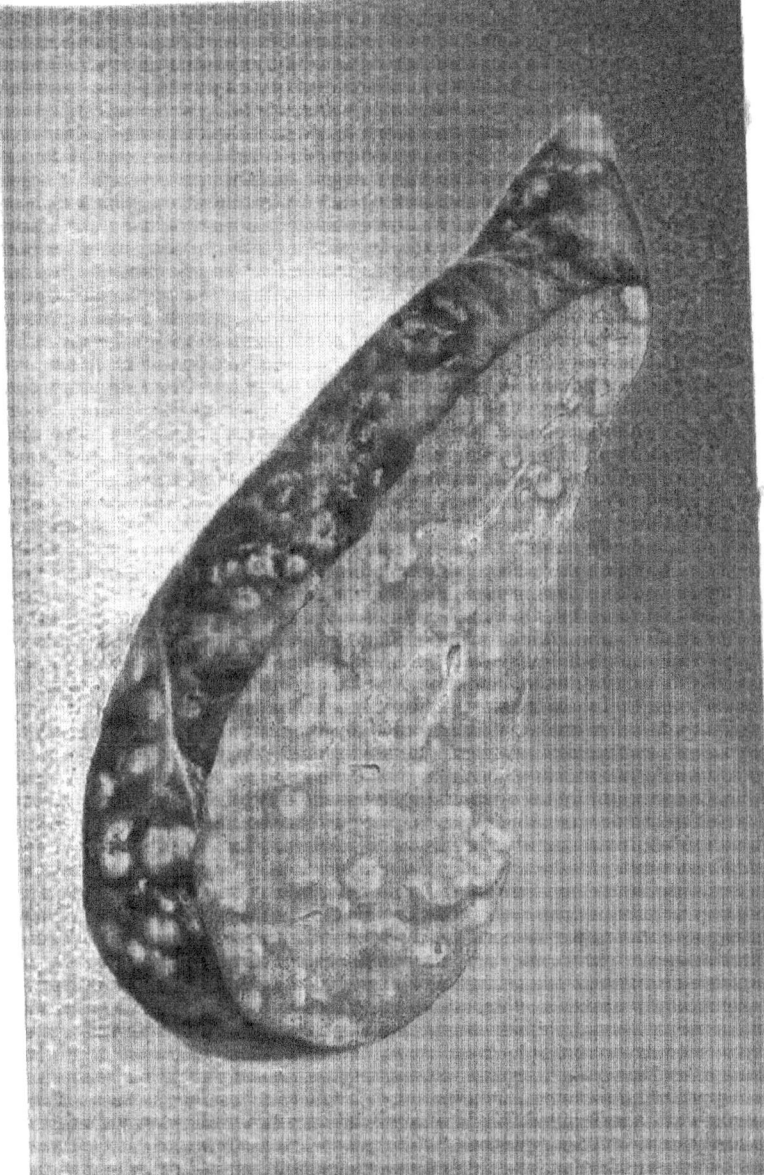

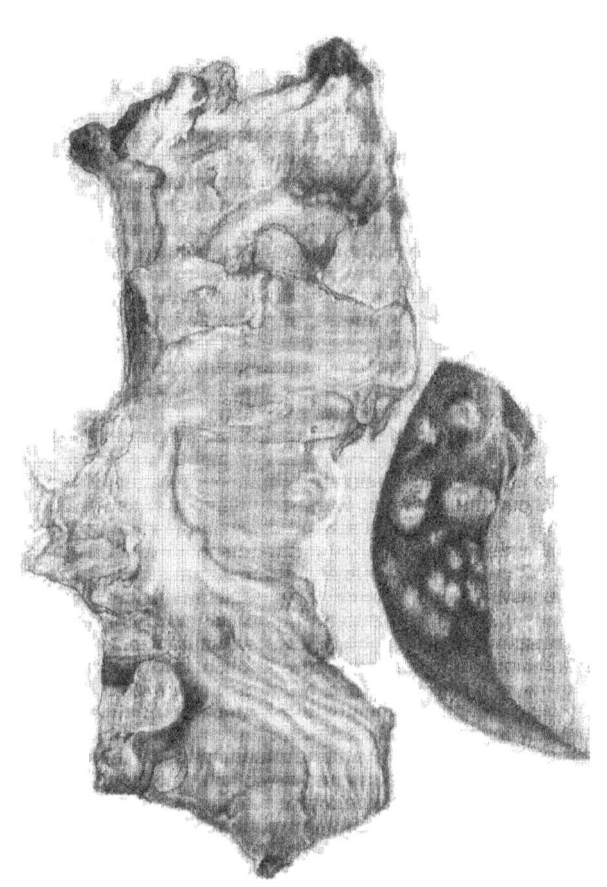

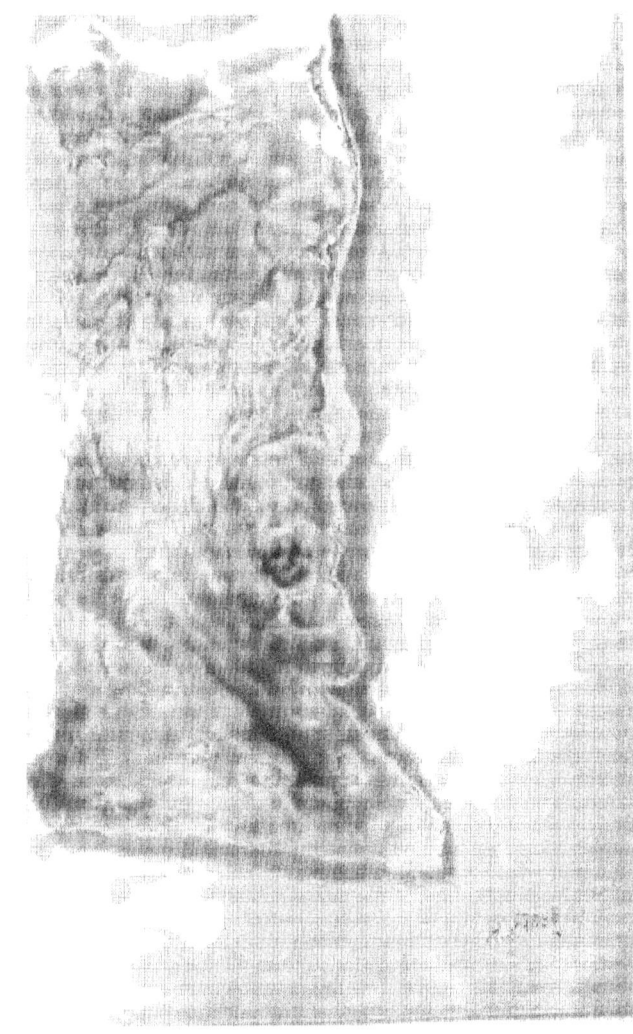

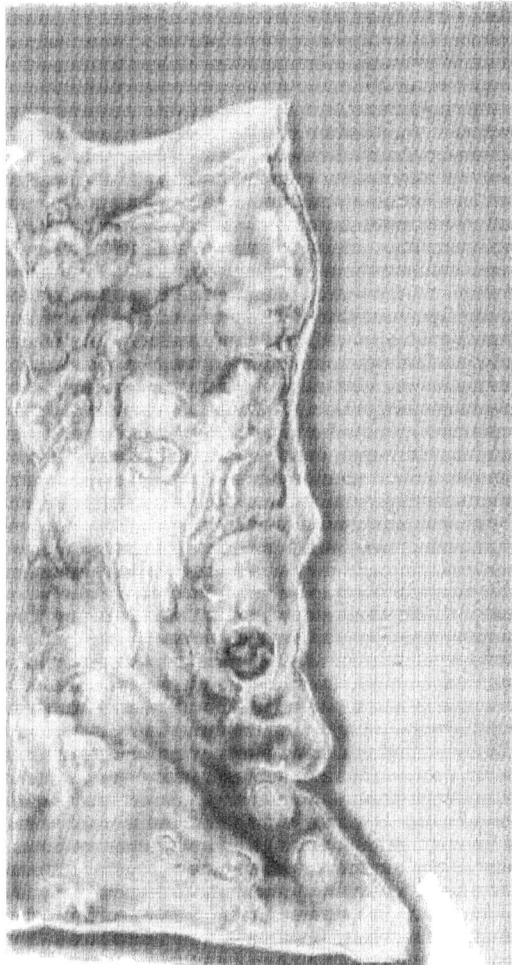

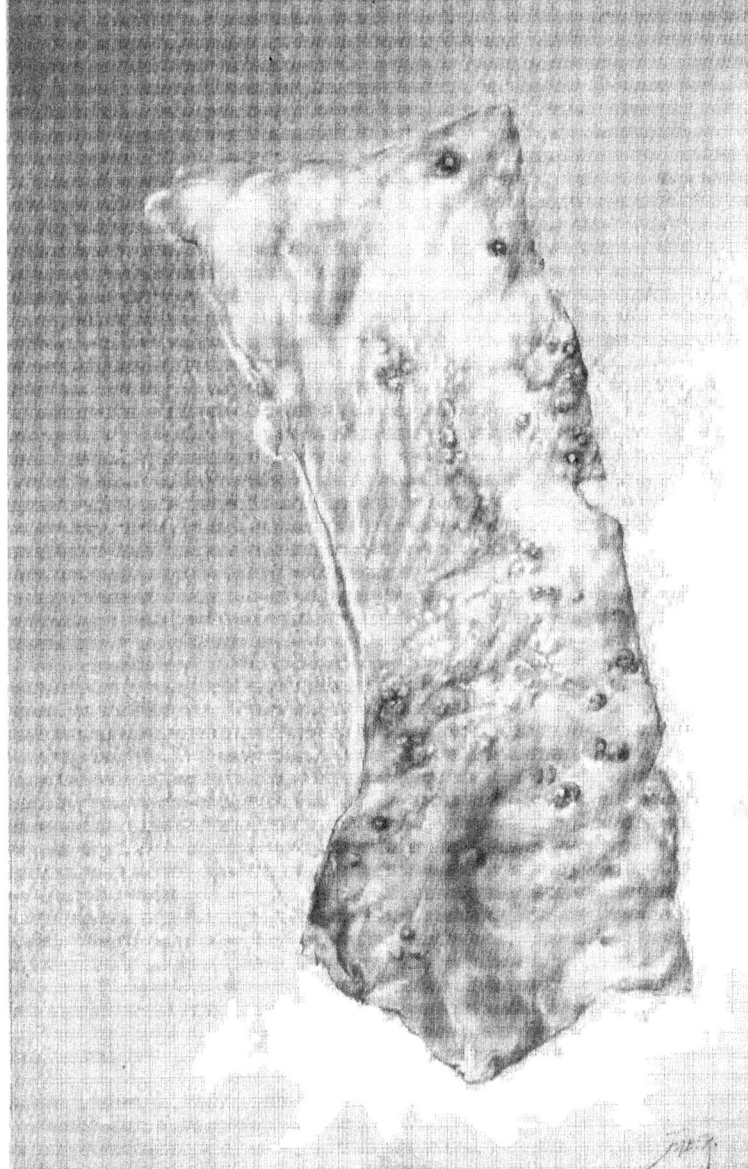

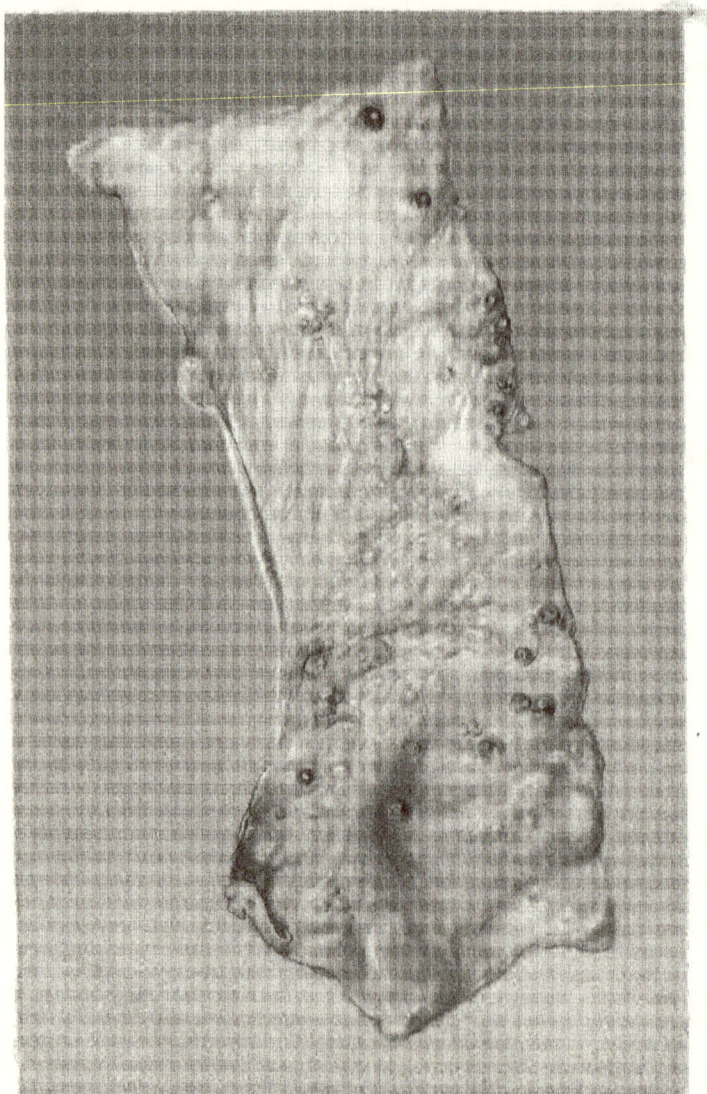

H. Faber pinx.                                                    F.Moras chromolith.Philad.

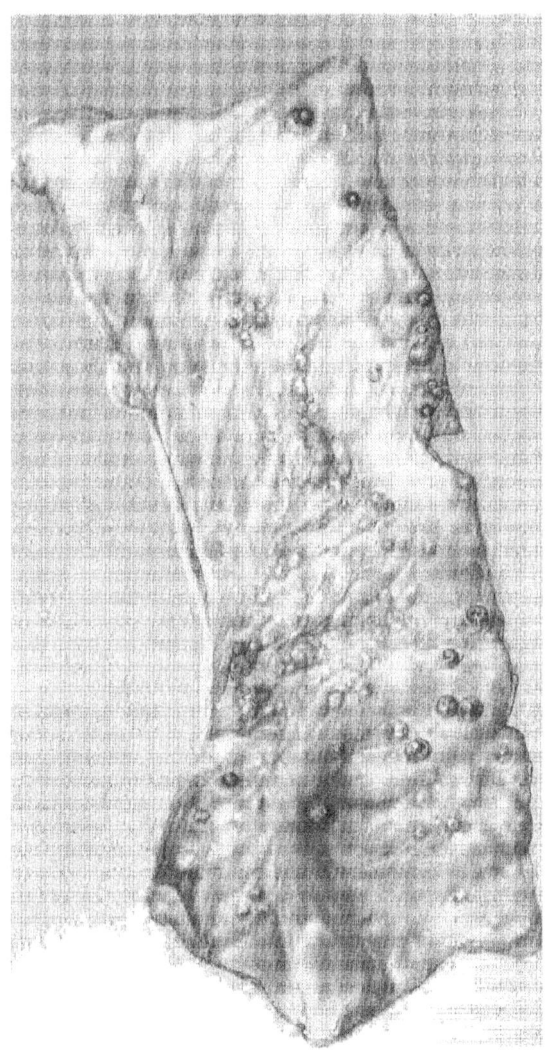

The color is thickened and anæmic.

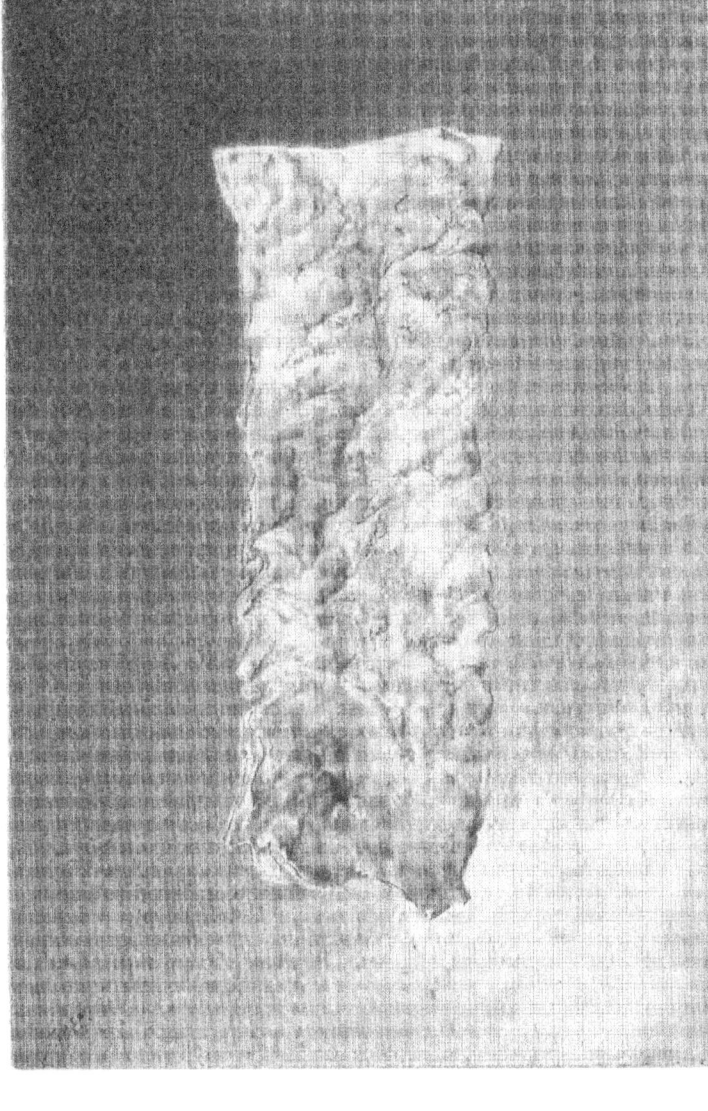

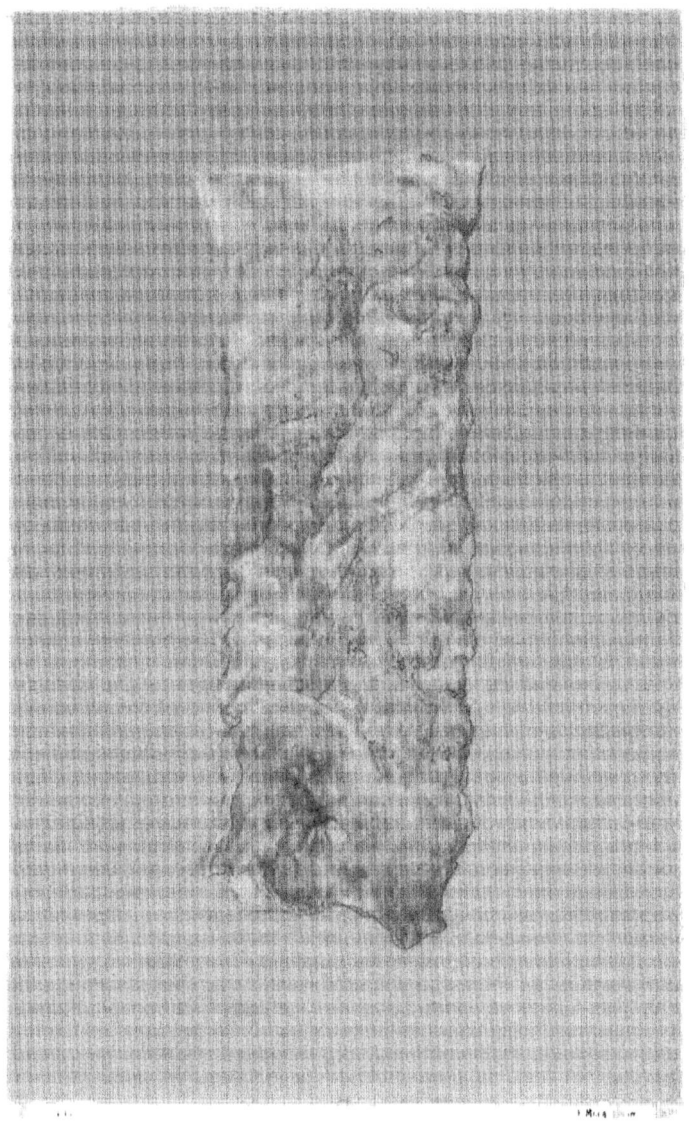

FOLLICULAR ULCERS OF COLON.—CHRONIC DYSENTERY.

The edges of many of the ulcers are fringed with pseudo-membrane

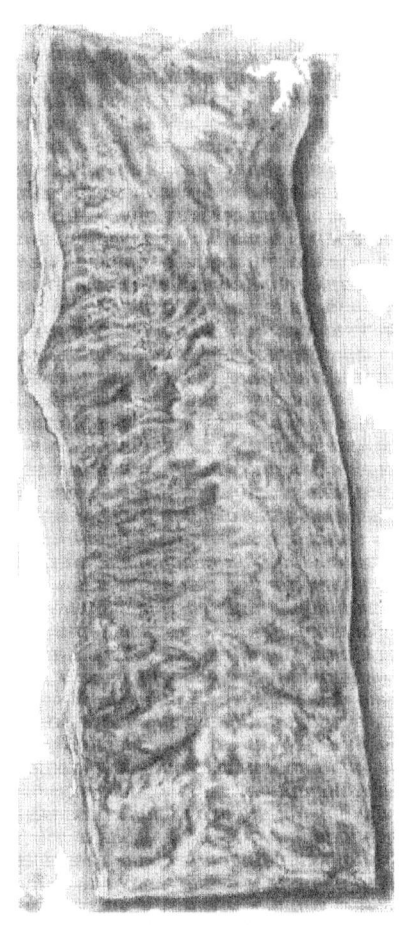

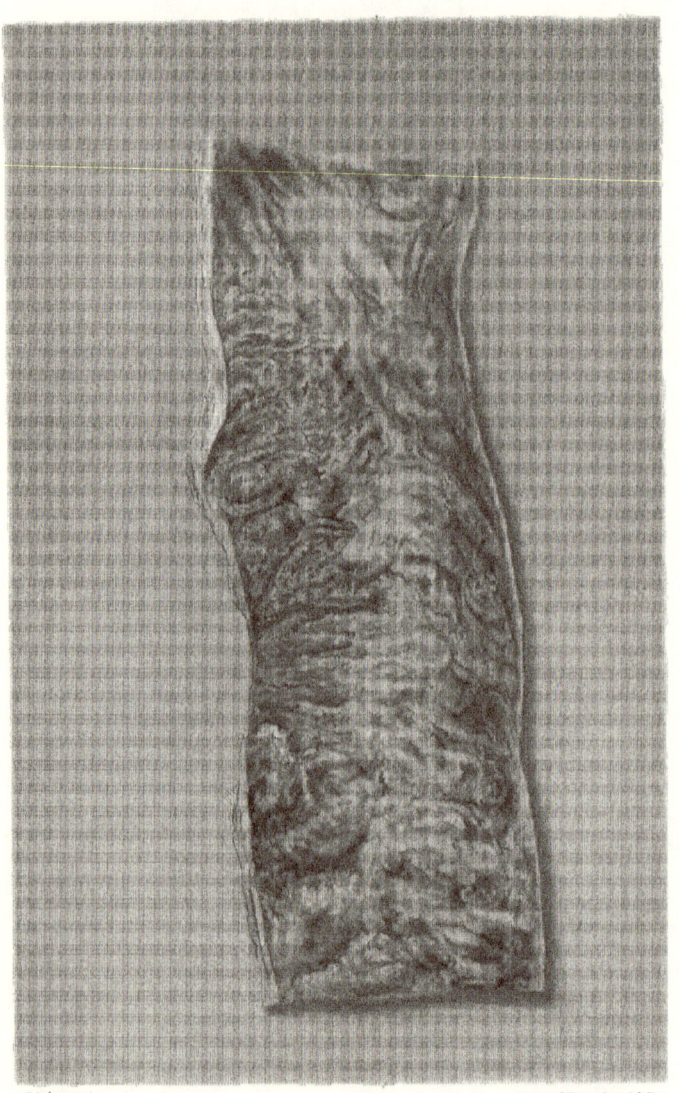

H Faber pinx.                                              F.Moras chromolith Phila

## PORTION OF DESCENDING COLON
with patches of pseudo membrane, and small ulcers.

PORTION OF DESCENDING COLON
with patches of pseudo membrane, and small ulcers.

# Originals

—of the—

—in CHROMOS the—

## THIRD MEDICAL VOLUME.

v. 1 pt 3

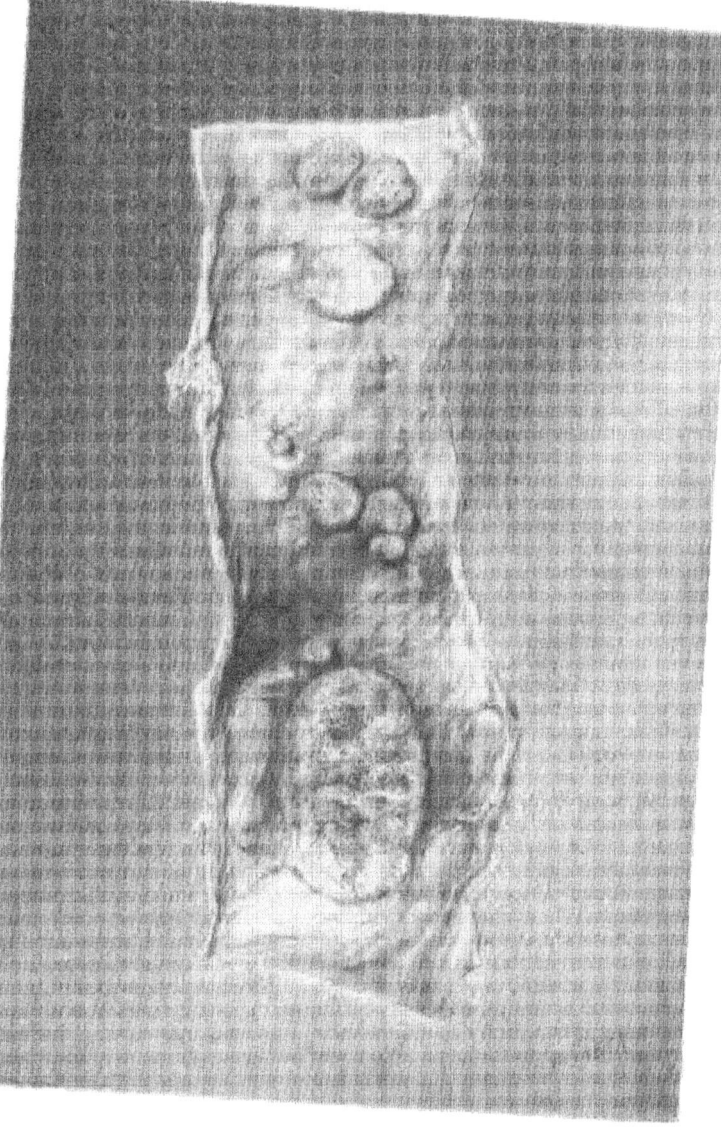

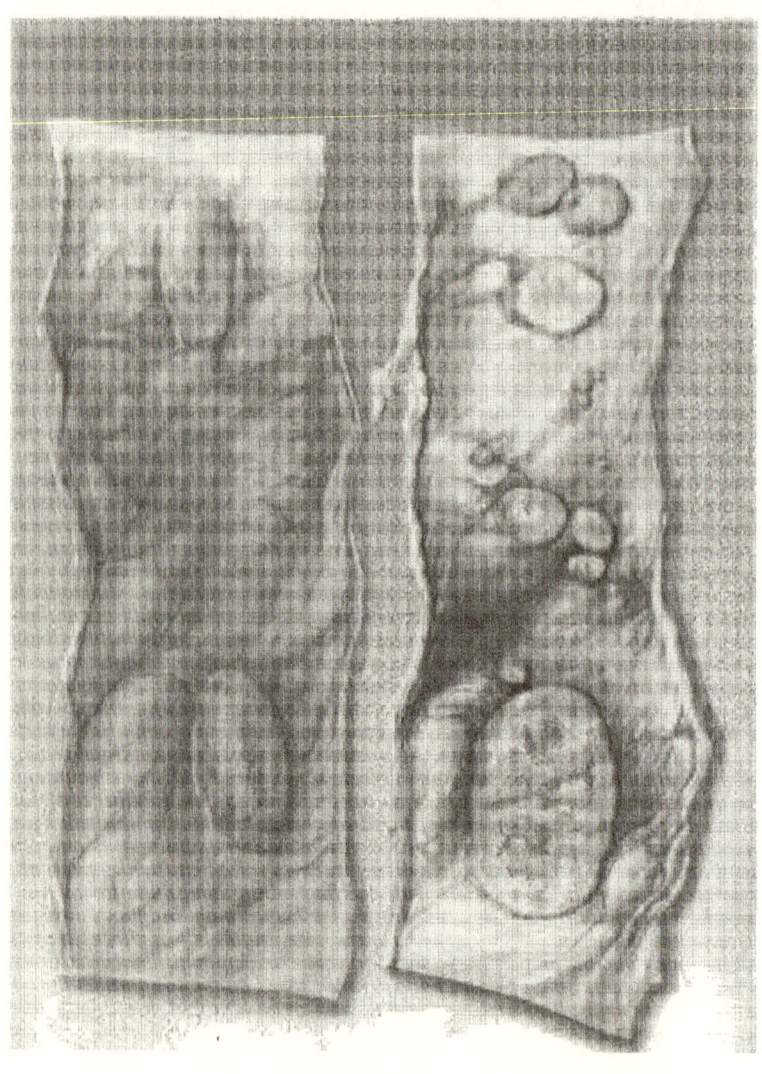

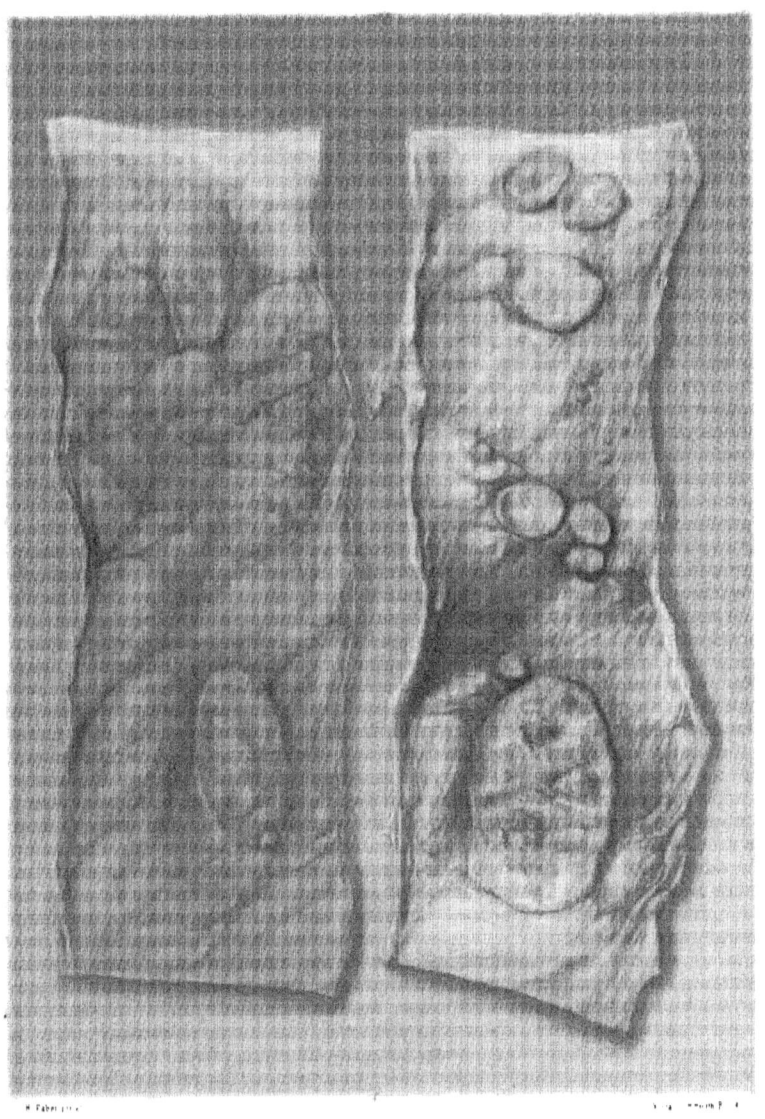

TYPHOID THICKENING OF PEYER'S PATCHES.

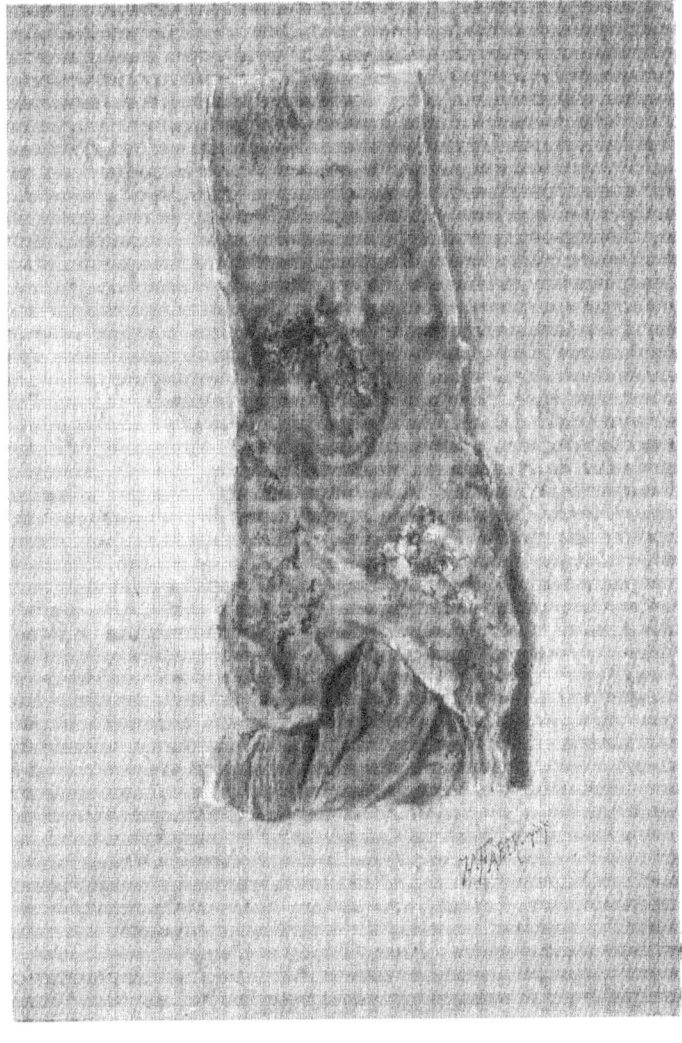

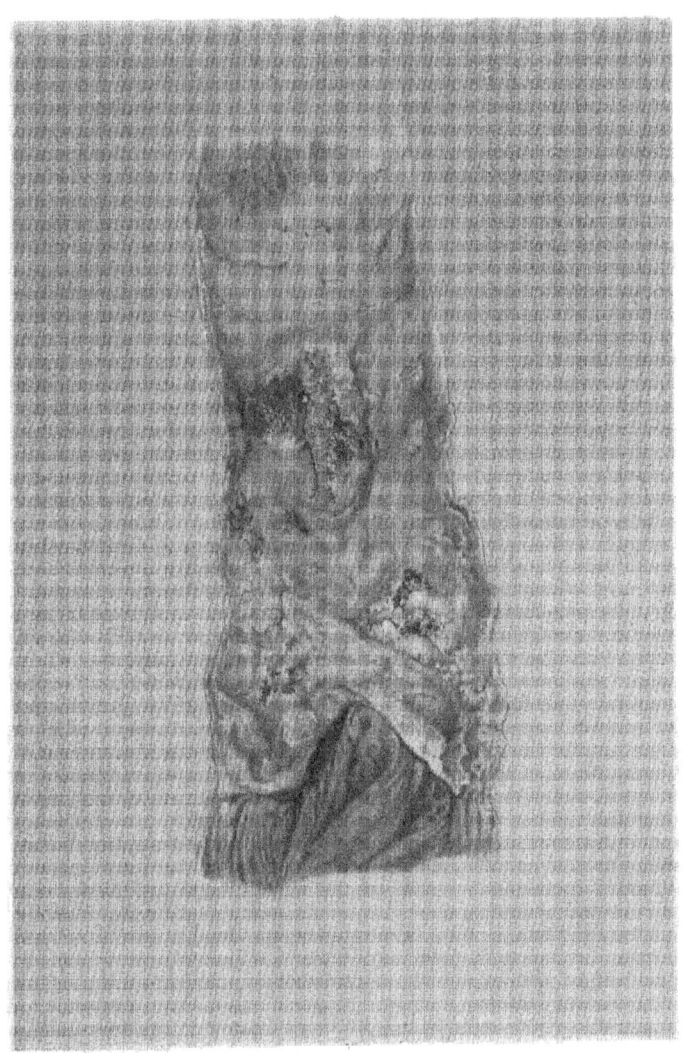

ULCERATED PEYER'S PATCH. FEVER
taken near the ileo-caecal valve.

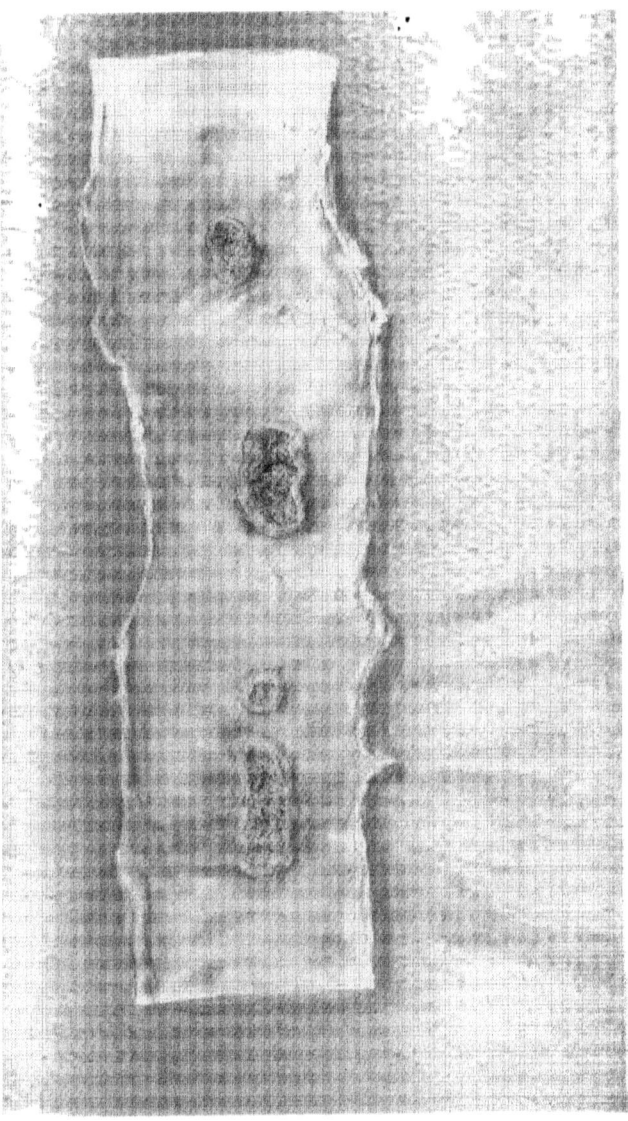

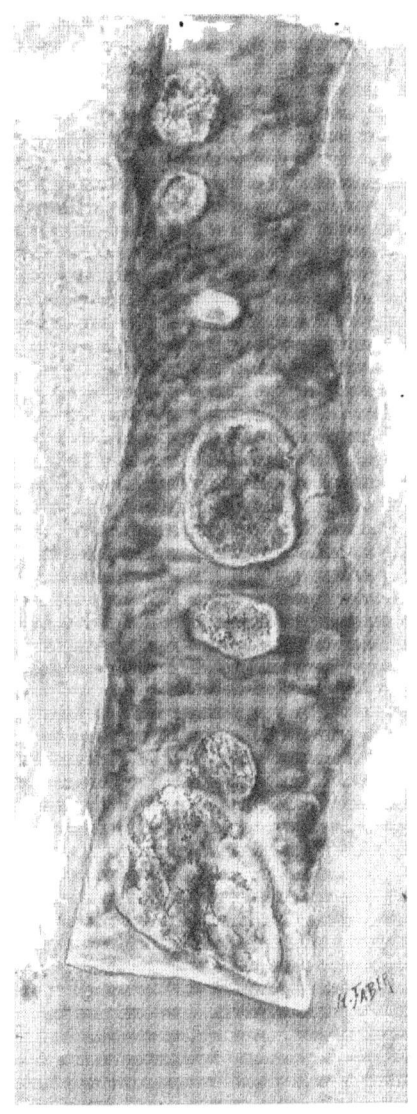

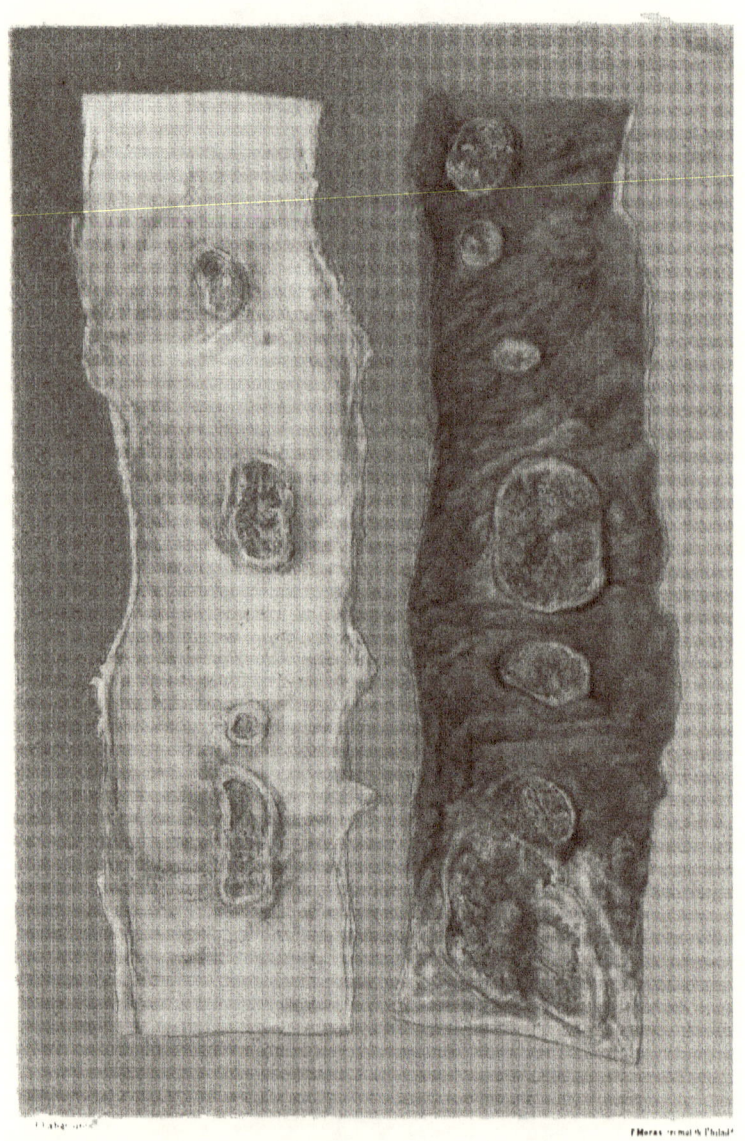

ULCERATED PEYER'S PATCHES.—FEVER.

The left piece from the upper, the right from the lower part of the ileum.

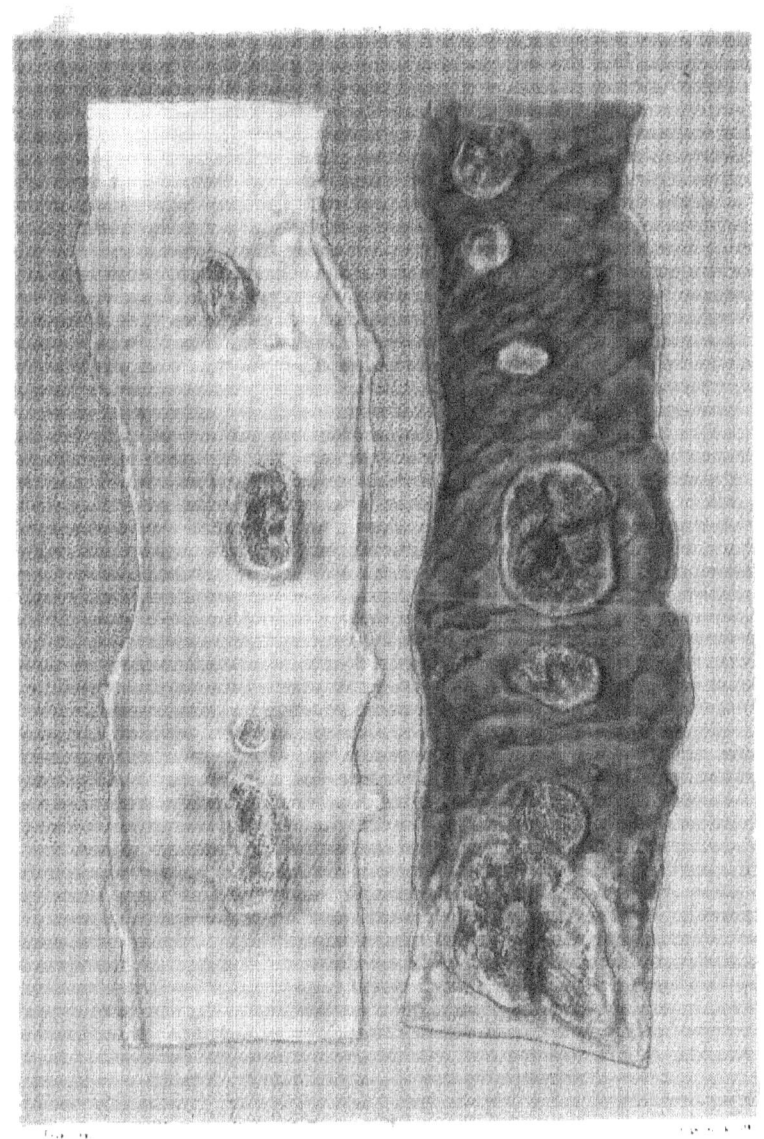

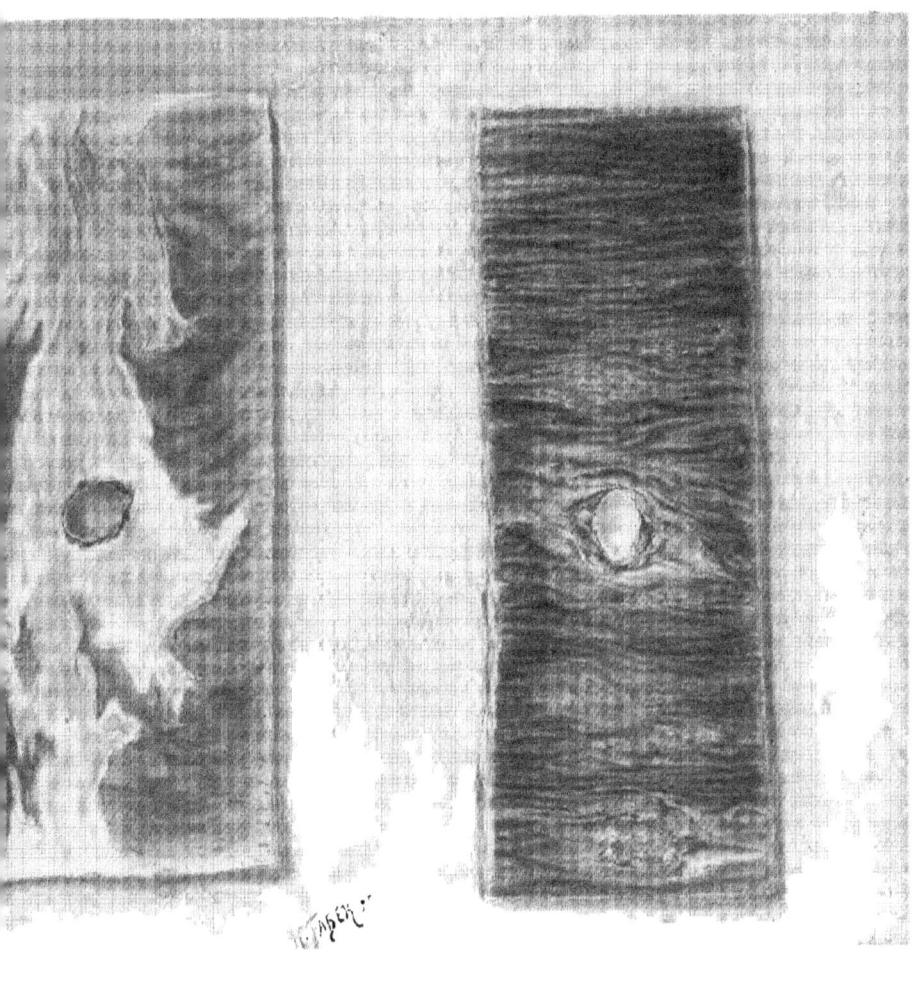

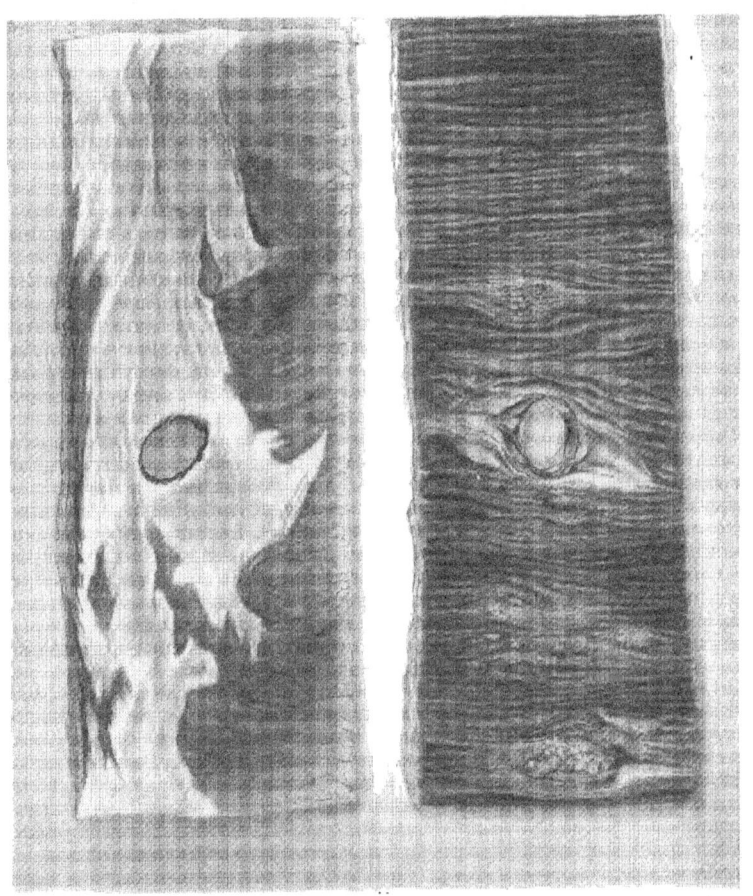

**PERFORATING ULCER OF THE ILEUM.**

The right hand piece shows the mucous, the left the peritoneal surface.

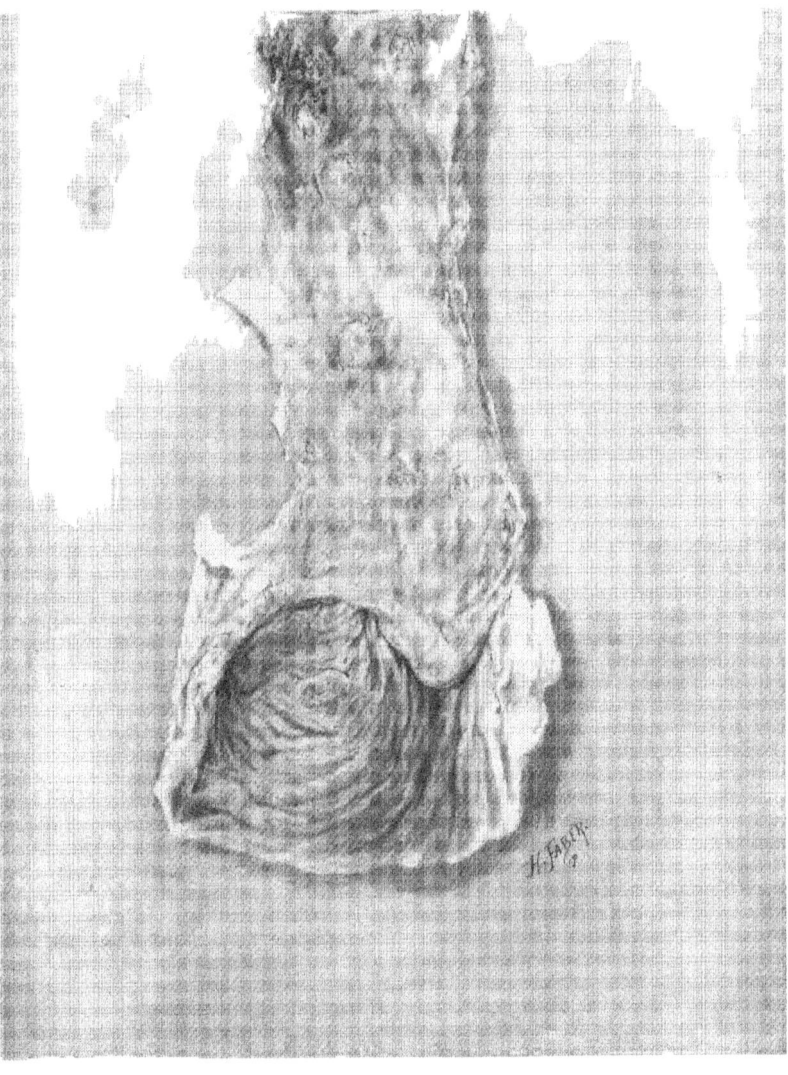

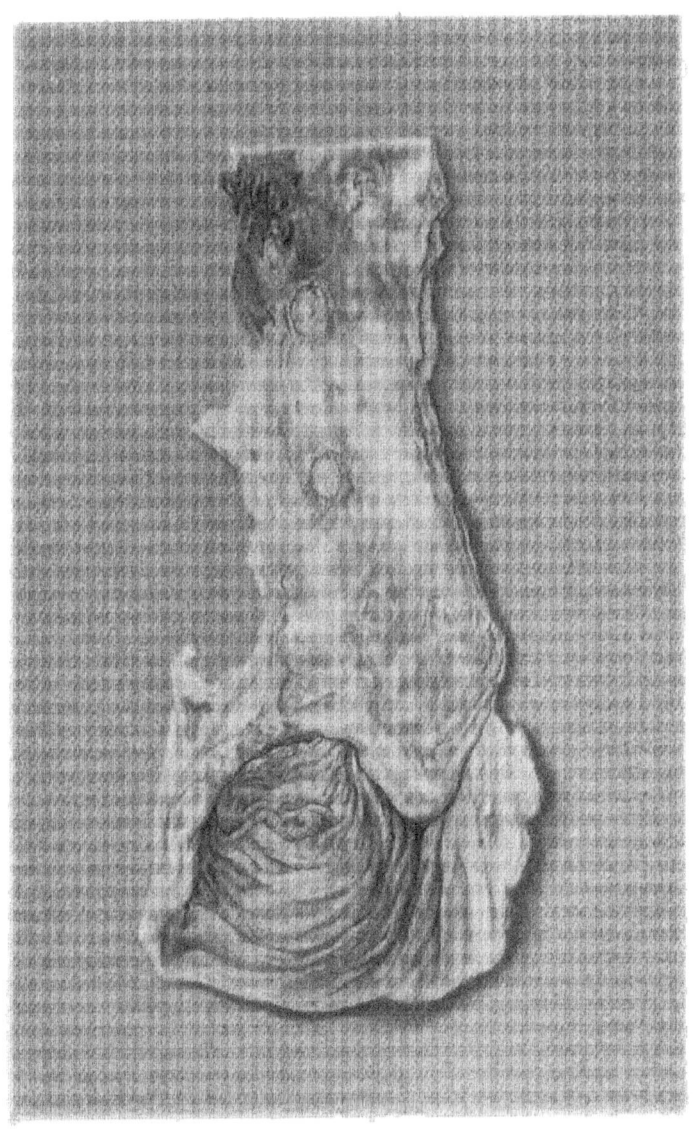

PERFORATION OF THE ILEUM, SPLEEN?